anythink

D0578735

cloverleaf books™

Off to School

Who Works at Hannah's School?

by **Lisa Bullard**

Illustrated by **Paula J. Becker**

M MILLBROOK PRESS • MINNEAPOLIS

For Robbie, the school bus driver
of every kid's dreams—L.B.

Millbrook Press
A division of Lerner Publishing Group, Inc.
241 First Avenue North
Minneapolis, MN 55401 USA

For reading levels and more information, look up this title at
www.lernerbooks.com.

Main body text set in Slappy Inline 22/28.
Typeface provided by T26.

Library of Congress Cataloging-in-Publication Data

Names: Bullard, Lisa, author.
Title: Who works at Hannah's school? / by Lisa Bullard ;
    Illustrated by Paula J. Becker.
Description: Minneapolis : Millbrook Press, 2017. | Series:
    Cloverleaf books—Off to school | Includes bibliographical
    references and index.
Identifiers: LCCN 2016038393 (print) | LCCN 2017009326
    (ebook) | ISBN 9781512439403 (lb : alk. paper) |
    ISBN 9781512451092 (eb pdf)
Subjects: LCSH: School employees—Juvenile literature. |
    Schools—Juvenile literature. | Students—Juvenile literature.
Classification: LCC LB2831.5 .B85 2017 (print) | LCC LB2831.5
    (ebook) | DDC 371.2/01—dc23
LC record available at https://lccn.loc.gov/2016038393

Manufactured in the United States of America
1-42153-25426-3/22/2017

TABLE OF CONTENTS

Chapter One

A Contest

My friend T.J. and I both broke our arms last week. He and I are going to see who can get the most new people to sign our casts today!

Mine already has lots of names,
so where am I going to find more?

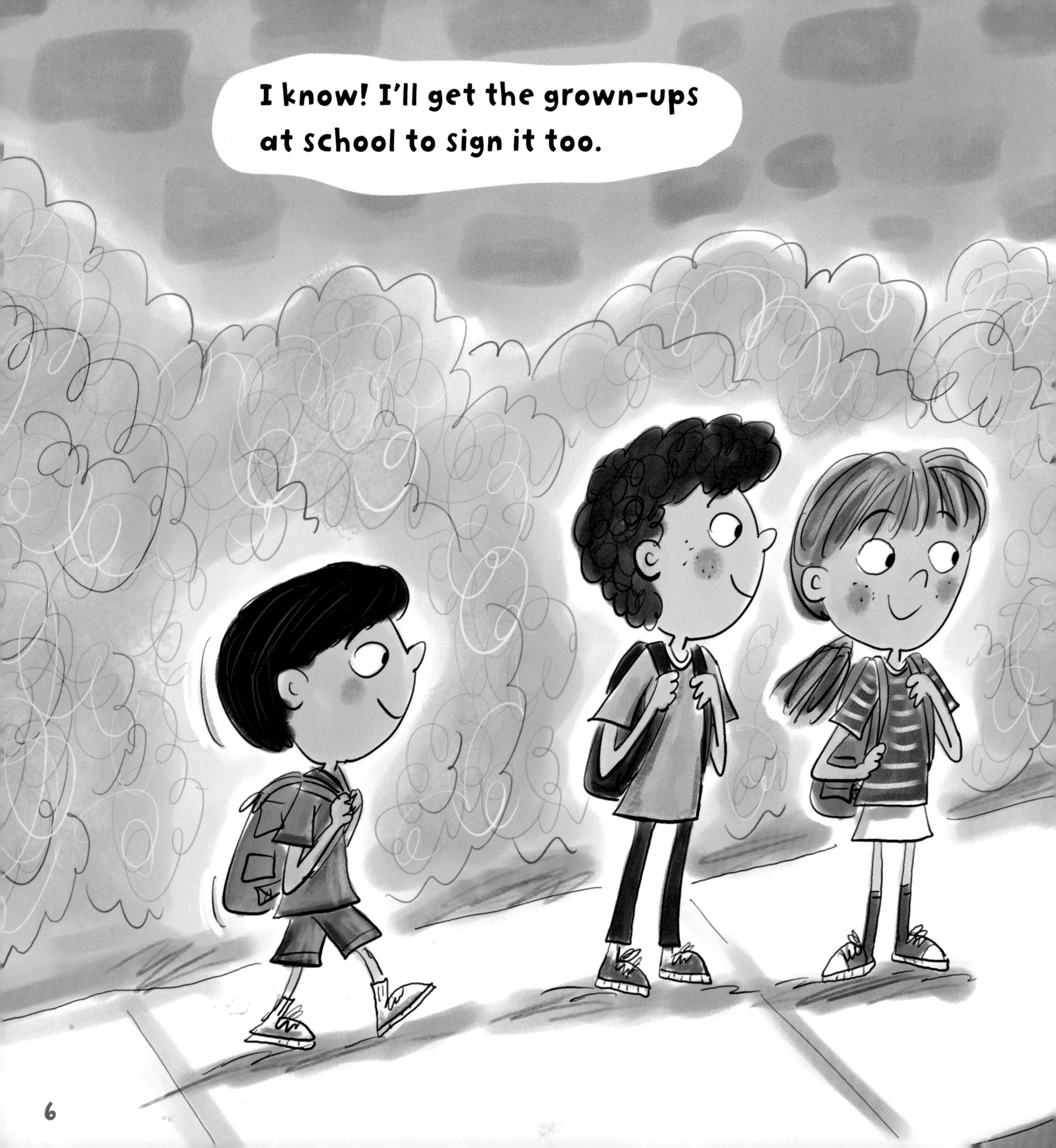
I know! I'll get the grown-ups at school to sign it too.

The crossing guard writes, "Safety first." I wish she'd said that *before* I broke my arm!

Crossing guards help students cross streets safely.

Mrs. Parsons, the school secretary,
drew a smiley face.

Principal Jennings writes, "Who's your pal?"

9

In My Classroom

José's grandma is our classroom volunteer. She draws a **heart**.

Some classrooms have helpers called paraprofessionals. Parents and grandparents often volunteer too.

And my classroom teacher,
Mr. Steinberg, gives me a gold star.

Around My School

Mr. Rodriguez adds a basketball sticker, Mrs. Lee paints a pretty picture, and Mr. Jones sketches a music note.

Crash! Mr. Louie the custodian is nice even when I drop my lunch tray. He signs my cast too!

The school nurse puts a bandage on my cast.

And Mrs. Grant, the librarian, lets me pick my favorite word out of the whole library. I choose *rainbow*!

I get extra help in reading from Ms. Young.

We're both proud that I can read everything on my cast!

19

Chapter Four

Time to Go Home

At the end of the day, T.J. and I compare our signatures.

It was so **fun** to talk to all the grown-ups
at school that it's **OK** that I didn't win.

21

When I Grow Up

There are many grown-ups who are helpers at school. Grown-ups also serve as helpers in other parts of your community. They include firefighters, safety officers, and youth leaders. Sometimes people do these jobs for pay. Sometimes they do them as volunteers. They all help make a strong community. What kind of helper would you like to be when you grow up?

What You Will Need
paper
pencil
coloring utensils

What You Will Do
Make a list of ideas of what kind of helper you want to be someday.
Draw a picture of yourself as a grown-up helping your community.

GLOSSARY

cast: a type of hard bandage that doctors put on a broken bone to help it heal

crossing guard: a person who helps children who are walking to and from school safely cross streets

custodian: a person who cleans and fixes problems in a building

librarian: a person in charge of a library

paraprofessional: a person whose job is helping teachers and students

principal: the person in charge of a school

secretary: someone who keeps records and organizes information

signature: the name of a person written by that person

volunteer: a person who does a job without being paid

BOOKS

Heos, Bridget. *Let's Meet a Teacher.* Minneapolis: Millbrook Press, 2013. See the many ways one teacher helps her students learn.

Marsico, Katie. *Working at a School.* Ann Arbor, MI: Cherry Lake, 2009. See photos and learn about the different jobs that grown-ups do at school.

Moreillon, Judi. *Ready and Waiting for You.* Grand Rapids, MI: Eerdmans Books for Young Readers, 2013. Read this fun story to see many different grown-ups at work in a school.

WEBSITES

School Helpers Help Out
https://www.teachervision.com/education-administration/school-helpers-help-out?downloadpdf=print
Do you remember which grown-up at school does what job? Use this matching activity to see how well you remember!

***Time for Kids:* Around the World**
http://www.timeforkids.com/around-the-world
Click on any country listed on this website, and then choose the "Day in the Life" option from the menu on the left. You will learn about what it is like to be a student in that country.

LERNER *e* SOURCE™
Expand learning beyond the printed book. Download free, complementary educational resources for this book from our website, www.lernerresource.com.